George W. Ward

**Notes in History**

Rome

George W. Ward

**Notes in History**
*Rome*

ISBN/EAN: 9783337381752

Printed in Europe, USA, Canada, Australia, Japan

Cover: Foto ©Andreas Hilbeck / pixelio.de

More available books at **www.hansebooks.com**

# NOTES IN HISTORY.

# ROME.

By GEORGE W. WARD, Ph.D.,

Professor of History and Politics,

WESTERN MARYLAND COLLEGE.

BALTIMORE, MD.:

Wm. J. C. DULANY COMPANY

# SELECTED ACCESSIBLE SOURCES.

1. LIVY.—Born B. C. 59 at Padua; lived at Rome; patronized by Augustus; died 17 A.D. Of the one hundred and forty-two books of Livy's History of Rome from the foundation of the city to the battle in Teutoburg Forest, 9 A.D., we have only thirty-five complete, the remainder, except two, in epitomes. Written for entertainment. Perfect style.

2. POLYBIUS.—Greek; born B. C. 204; taken to Rome among the one thousand hostages after the battle of Pydna, patronized by Scipio with whom he was present at the destruction of Carthage, Corinth, and Numantia (?); died B. C. 122. Of the forty books of Polybius's History [Pragmeteia] we have only five complete. Nearly contemporaneous source for the Second Punic War—followed here by Livy. History of Rome's world conquest. Written for instruction. Poor style.

3. DIONYSIUS of Halicarnassus.—Came to Rome B. C. 29, where he remained till his death B. C. 7. Of the twenty-two books of Dionysius, we possess eleven—these come down only to B. C. 441—just after the Twelve Tables. Minute early history to teach his people the greatness of Rome. Full of speeches—rhetoric rather than history.

4. CICERO.—One of the ablest men produced by Rome. A very voluminous writer. Besides their historical value his orations are among the best specimens of oratory in existence. No man of his age did more to preserve the liberties of Rome. Read especially the four orations against Cataline.

5. CÆSAR.—History of the first seven years of the Gallic Wars in seven books, and of the Civil War in three books. The eighth book of the Gallic Wars and the last three books of the Civil War are by another hand—Hirtius (?) Contemporary source.

6. PLUTARCH.—Born at Chaeronea in Boeotia shortly before 50 A. D. (?); was a student of philosophy when Nero made his tour of Greece in 66 A. D. Forty-six Parallel Lives—a Greek, then a Roman, then a comparison.

7. TACITUS.—Born shortly before 61 A. D.; patronized by the Flavian emperors and by Nerva and Trajan; died soon after 117 A. D. Voluminous writer. Of Tacitus's historical works the Agricola [Life of his father-in-law] and the Germania (description of Germany and the Germans) have come down to us complete. Of the history we have only four books complete covering only one year [Galba, Otho, and Vitellius], and a fragment of the fifth book to the siege of Jerusalem. Of the sixteen books of the Annales, the fifth, seventh, eighth, ninth, tenth, and parts of the eleventh and sixteenth books are lost. Contemporary source except the Annales which deal with the generation just preceding his own.

8. SUETONIUS.—Contemporary with Tacitus. Lives of the Twelve Cæsars [Julius Cæsar to Domitian, 96 A. D.]

9. AMMIANUS MARCELLINUS.—Greek; native of Antioch; early joined the Imperial Body-guards and served under Julian (361-363 A. D.) Of the thirty-one books of his History of Rome from Nerva 96 A. D. to Valens, 378 A. D., the first thirteen are lost. The part extant is a contemporaneous source.

# ROME.

## PART I.—THE MONARCHY.

### LECTURE I. GEOGRAPHY, RELIGION, ETHNOGRAPHY.

1. SITUATION.—With a good map in hand notice that the Italian peninsula lies northwest of Greece. To the South lies Sicily, separated from the mainland by the Strait of Messina [Scylla and Charybdis]. The Adriatic sea lies east, while the shores south and west are washed by the Mediterranean.

1. TOPOGRAPHY.—In shape the peninsula has been compared to a boot, the heel directed toward Greece, the toe toward Sicily. In the north, between the Alps and the northern spurs of the Apennines lies the valley of the Po. Stretching thence south-easterly, through the entire length of the Peninsula, are the Apennines, a backbone of mountain nowhere more than two thousand feet high. On each side, a narrow plain traversed by a few small streams, lies between the base of the mountains and the shore. The Tiber falls into the western sea opposite Southern Corsica.

3. Draw from memory an outline map of Italy, and locate (1) Po; (2) Arno; (3) Tiber; (4) Rubicon; (5) Metaurus; (6) Vulturnus; (7) Aufidus; (8) Rome; (9) Capua; (10) Cannae; (11) Tarentum; (12) Beneventum; (13) Ostia; (14) Veii; (15) Lake Trasimenus; (16) Via Appia; (17) Via Flaminia.

4. RELIGION.—In Rome, as in Greece, there was little distinction between church and state. The king was also high priest, conducting the national ceremonies, performing the national sacrifices. No political act of importance could be undertaken without first consulting the auspices.

5. GODS.—(1) Jupiter, "father of gods and men;" (2) Mars, war, legendary father of the *Populus Romanus;* (3) Saturn, agriculture; (4) Neptune, the sea; (5) Hercules, gain; (6) Mercury, traffic. Ihne's Early Rome., VI.

6. GODDESSES.—(1) Juno, wife of Jupiter; (2) Venus, love; (3) Minerva, wisdom; (4) Vesta, national hearth; (5) Ceres, agriculture; (6) Ops, harvest and wealth.

7. SACRED COLLEGES.—(1) Pontiffs, highest religious power; head, pontifex maximus; decided days for public business, thus becoming a tool in the hands of the government. [4, then 9, then 16]. (2) Augurs, [4, 9, 16] consulted will of gods by omens; (3) Heralds, [20] treaties, war, ambassadors; (4) Keepers of the Sibylline Books [Duumviri Sacrorum] of Etruscan origin; Sibyl offered to sell books, first nine, then six, then three, which were bought.

8. ETHNOGRAPHY.—Indo-European—Aryan. The first historical name in Italy is that of the "Siculi," a people who have left themselves a monument in the name "Sicily." A tribe apparently contemporaneous with them was the Ligures. These were overthrown by the Pelasgi and the Aborigines. Of both these peoples some remains may still be traced. Later still, we find the Etruscans north, the Latins and Sabines south of the Tiber. The Latins and the Sabines were separated by the Anio.

## LECTURE II.  THE PRIMITIVE ROMAN STATE.

1. CHARACTER OF THE LEGENDS.—The first three-and-a-half centuries of Roman history may be regarded as traditional.  "What little we do know is mainly derived from inference."  But the legends are interesting and contain, no doubt, a fairly accurate picture of Roman life and institutions in the earliest times.  Read the legends themselves; no digest can convey any fair idea of their interest or their importance as an institutional study.

2. TRADITION points to an aboriginal race in Itlay, reinforced after the Trojan war by wanderers from Troy [Æneas] and immigrants from Greece [Evander].  Another legend makes Romulus the founder of the city, which afterwards took its name from him.  The Sabines claimed to be a colony from Sparta.  Plutarch.  Ihne's *Early Rome*, Ch. II.

3. STORY OF ROMULUS [and Remus].—Descended from Æneas, son of Mars, and a Vestal, exposed by their uncle, suckled by a wolf, rescued by Faustulus, identified in a quarrel [about cattle?], and their usurping uncle overthrown.  They then move across the Tiber to the Palatine [spot where they were washed ashore?], take the auspices, decide to build on the site chosen by Romulus; Remus killed in a quarrel, and the city called from the shape of the Palatine, "Roma Quadrata," Square Rome.

4. THE REIGN OF ROMULUS —Romulus opened his city to robbers and all the rough characters of surrounding tribes [Asylum].  Thus the population increased apace; but there were no women.  To remedy this a feast was arranged to which the neighboring Sabines were invited.  At a signal, the Romans rush upon the Sabine daughters, each securing for himself a wife.  The Sabine fathers make war; in the midst of a doubtful battle the captured daughters go out and plead for peace, as, in any case, it must be their husbands or their fathers who are defeated.  Peace arranged.  [Rape of the Sabine Women.  Tarpeia].

5. CONSTITUTION OF PRIMITIVE ROME.—(1) The people were divided into three tribes, Ramnes [Romans], Tities (tish-i-es) [Sabines], and Luceres [mixed].  (2) The government was carried on through a Senate and Comitia Curiata, afterwards Centuriata.  Ihne's *Early Rome*, V.    (3) The classes in the state were Patricians, Clients, Slaves and Plebians.

6. THE KING was general in war, judge in peace, and always high-priest of the nation.  Ihne's *Early Rome*, VII.

7. THE SENATE was not a law-making, but merely an influential advisory body.  In theory it consisted of the "fathers" [patres] in Rome.  The head of each clan [family] was, upon appointment of the king, a member of the Senate.  Ihne's *Early Rome*, Ch. VIII.

8. THE COMITIA CURIATA was an assembly of the members of the curiae, each curia having one vote on such matters as the king chose to lay before them.  The duties of this body gradually passed to the Centuriata.

## LECTURE III.  NUMA, TULLUS HOSTILIUS, AND ANCUS MARCIUS.

1. ELECTION OF NUMA.—Upon the apotheosis of Romulus there was no one to succeed him.  The senators agreed to perform the office of king by turns, each serving only one day and night [Interregnum].  The restless, pugnacious Romans soon tired of this oligarchical rule and insisted upon having a king.  At last it was agreed by the Romans and Sabines [Lect. II., 3] that a king should be chosen out of one tribe by the people of the other tribe.  The Romans preferred the right of choice to that of furnishing a king, and Numa was chosen from the Sabine City of Cures.

2. NOTIFICATION.—Numa lived in quiet retirement, and, after the death of his wife habitually sought solitude and the company of a deity, from whom he received wisdom Thus he had reached his fortieth year when ambassadors came from Rome to make him king. Numa declined the honor, but was afterwards persuaded by his father to accept.

3. CORONATION.—Numa was a strikingly handsome, athletic figure, which greatly delighted the Romans. Met by Senate and people they proceeded to the capitol. The chief of Augurs covered Numa's head, turned his face to the south, and with his right hand on Numa's head waited for some sign from the gods. Soon "the auspicious birds appeared and passed by on the right hand. Then Numa took the royal robe and went down from the mount to the people, who received him with loud acclammations as the most pious of men and most beloved of the gods."

4. NUMA'S REIGN.—Numa was a lawgiver, the second founder of the Roman State. He devoted himself to the arts of peace and to religion. He discharged the guard of soldiers which had protected Romulus, reorganized the priesthood, founded the College of Pontiffs [Lect. I., 7], established the order of Vestal Virgins and the sacred fire. [See Plutarch's Numa, p. 634], and the College of Heralds [Lect. I., 7]. Numa blotted out the jealousy between Romans and Sabines by classifying the people by trades: "Musicians, goldsmiths, masons, dyers, shoemakers, tanners, braziers, and potters;" and "collected the other artificers also into companies, who had their respective halls, courts, and religious ceremonies peculiar to each society." He repealed the law permitting parents to sell their children, reformed the calendar, and died in a good old age, leaving the Romans peaceful and prosperous. Plutarch's *Numa*.

5. TULLUS HOSTILIUS.—Aped Romulus, conquered Alba—Horatii and Curiatii. [See Livy 1., 22-26]. Defeated Fidenae and Veii, destroyed Alba and tore asunder with chariots the body of the Alban king. Later became remorseful, but upon approaching Jupiter the offended god struck him dead with lightning.

6. ANCUS MARCIUS.—Grandson of Numa and less warlike than Hostilius. He conquered the Latins and established a colony of them on the Aventine. These were the originals plebs. Founded Ostia at the mouth of the Tiber, fortified the Janiculum and connected it with Rome by a bridge.

### LECTURE IV. TARQUINIUS PRISCUS, SERVIUS, AND TARQUINIUS SUPERBUS.

1. THE HISTORICAL KINGS.—It is usually believed that while the stories of the first four kings are entirely fabulous, those of the last contain much that is historical. But there is much of fable mixed with whatever truth there may be in the accounts of even the last three. It may perhaps be confidently affirmed that Rome, like most primitive states, was founded a kingdom. But not even the course of her history may be certainly made out till the kingdom is changed into a republic.

2. THE ETRUSCAN LINE.—Tarquinius Priscus was the son of Demaratus, a noble of Corinth, who, when tyranny was established there fled to Etruria. Tarquin married an influential princess of Etruria, but, being an alien, was kept out of power and was finally persuaded by his wife to go to Rome. Here he gained rapidly in popularity with both people and senate. Upon the death of Ancus Marcius, Tarquin was unanimously elected to the throne. Thus were the Etruscan princess established at Rome.

3. TARQUIN'S REIGN.—The Etruscans proved to be powerful rulers. Under Tarquin Rome sprang forward almost as if by magic. The Latins and Etruscans were defeated and the town of Collatia was taken from the Sabines. The lower, swampy part of the city was drained—Cloaca Maxima—the Circus Maximus laid out and the Roman Games instituted; the Forum was laid out and adorned, while a great temple to Jupiter was built on the Capitoline, and a wall around the city begun. Tarquin added the third tribe—Luceres—to the state, and the third hundred to the senate.

Then he doubled the number of members in each·tribe. After a brilliant reign of thirty-eight years he was assassinated by sons of Ancus Marcius. His successor, Servius Tullius, was reputed to have been born a slave.

4. SERVIUS TULLIUS.—Servius had been the favorite of queen Tanaquil, and upon the murder of Tarquin [which she at first concealed] Servius was produced as king without consent of the popular assemblies. Servius, though irregularly chosen king, did more than almost any other king to shape the future of Rome. He was a great builder. During his reign, the city for the first time included all the seven hills, and was entirely enclosed by a wall. This was but little changed in five hundred years. He re-organized the state on a military basis, and from that time for almost a thousand years the Roman army was one of the main factors in the complicated movement of world history. He distributed conquered lands among the poor. Nobles complain. Servius assassinated.

5. THE SERVIAN CONSTITUTION.—Except the senate, Servius changed the Constitution from the basis of birth to that of wealth. This important change was effected through the army, and was not complete till long after the death of its author. What Servius actually did was thoroughly to reorganize the army. He made it to consist of one hundred and seventy-five centuries of foot, and eighteen centuries of horse. The levies and the voting were according to wealth. [Plebeians]. Voting took place in the Centuriata, where questions of war and foreign policy were decided—next to the senate the most powerful body in the State. [Thirty Plebeian tribes created.]

6. TARQUINIUS SUPERBUS.—The last of the Roman kings came to the throne through the influence of his wife, Tullia. She effected her purpose by the murder of her first husband, her sister, and finally of her father, the king over whose mangled body she drove her chariot in the street hence named Sceleratus. On the throne Tarquin proved to be as great as he was wicked. Under him Rome first became the acknowledged leader among a number of neighboring nations. [He carried the Roman arms further than any predecessor had done, besides completing the great works begun by Servius]. Became oppressive; compelled to flee on account of his son's outrage to Lucretia. Plutarch's *Publicola*.

7. CRITICISM OF THE LEGENDS.—The stories told by Livy, Plutarch and others, of the foundling of Rome and the reign of the first four kings, it must be remembered are very questionable authorities if, indeed, they are not wholly creations of the imagination. Rome, with all its records, (?) was burned B. C., 390, by the Gauls. With the exception of a few laws, a few family histories, and the annals of Fabius Pictor, upon which Livy appears to have relied to a great extent, we possess little of the history of Rome that was not written from two hundred to five hundred years after the events narrated.

## PART II.—THE REPUBLIC, B. C. 510–31.

### SECTION I.—ROME ON HER SEVEN HILLS (510–343).

#### LECTURE V.  EARLY DAYS OF THE REPUBLIC.

1. TARQUIN ATTEMPS TO REGAIN THE THRONE.—Driven from Rome by force, Tarquin soon collected an army and returned to fight for his throne. In the battle which followed neither party won a decisive victory, but the king's son killed Brutus, the defilement of whose wife, Lucretia, had led to the overthrow of Tarquin. The Roman women mourned for Brutus a whole year.

2. LARS PORSENA.—Tarquin now turned to his kindred, the Etrurians. Porsena was their most powerful king. Listening to Tarquin's appeal, he led a force toward Rome. The Senate was seized with terror, and granted great privileges to the people in order to unite them against the enemy. Across the Sublician bridge the Romans marched to the Janiculum, and there awaited the enemy.

3. HORATIUS AT THE BRIDGE.—Porsena and his Tuscans, by a sudden assault, drove the Romans in confusion from their position. The bridge now offered to the Romans their only means of escape, to Porsena, the only passage into Rome. In the midst of the rout Horatius Cocles called in vain upon the Romans to make a stand, and, finally, with only two companions, himself took position at the bridge. Porsena was checked till the Romans could cross and destroy the bridge, after the two companions had crossed on a fragment. Then Horatius, with a prayer to "Father Tiberinus," threw himself in full armor into the river, and amidst a shower of missiles swam safe to the Roman side—"an act which is likely to obtain more fame than credit with posterity." [Livy. I., 9, 10].

4. MUCIUS SCAEVOLA.—Porsena now sent for boats to guard the river, and effected a siege of Rome. The Romans were soon distressed and attempted to relieve the city by an ambush. Only a few of Porsena's men were taken, however, and the siege continued. Then three hundred Roman youths made a plot to assassinate Porsena. The lot fell first upon Mucius. Having gone in disguise to Porsena's camp, he was unable to distinguish the king from his secretary, who sat in similar dress beside him. The blow fell upon the secretary, and Mucius was captured. Porsena had fires built around and then ordered Mucius to tell about the plot. Instead of doing so, Mucius thrust his right hand into the fire, where it was soon burned off before the king's eyes. The king was so struck with his bravery that he dismissed Mucius with honor—afterwards called Scaevola, the "left-handed."

5. THE CONSULS.—Porsena now retired, and the Romans proceeded to choose for their ruler, not a king—they had vowed never again to allow a king in Rome—but two consuls who were jointly to share most of the king's duties. [Copied from the Spartans? See "The Eastern Civilizations and Greece," Lect. IX., 2]. This was, perhaps, the only difference between the kingdom and the republic, except that the consuls were chosen by both patricians and plebeians in the Centuriata; the kings had been chosen by the patricians alone in the Curiata. The defect was that one could veto the act of the other. The revolution rather *opened the way* for great changes than *made* them

6. THE DICTATOR, B. C., 501.—This was an extraordinary and occasional officer who might be, under urgent necessity—usually war—appointed by decree of the Senate through the consul, for six months, at the end of which time he must retire to private life—[Cf. the "Tyrant" in Greek politics, "The Eastern Civilizations and Greece," Lect. XI., 4-5]. The Dictator stood above law. Absolutely supreme, he could give unity and effectiveness to military operations such as could be secured in no other way. Almost immediately upon the establishment of the Republic a Dictator was appointed to make the executive power respected by all parties. Story of the dictatorship of Cincinnatus?

## LECTURE VI. PATRICIANS AND PLEBEIANS.

1. BATTLE OF LAKE REGILLUS.—The Latins, being about to make war on Rome, were joined by the Tarquins. The hostile forces met at Lake Regillus, where Tarquinius Superbus, himself now an old man, fought valiantly against Rome. This proved to be the bloodiest battle the Romans had yet fought. Spite against the Tarquins led to bloody personal encounters, and the battle—finally won by the Romans in an impetuous charge upon the enemies' camp—became the proverb of severity for future ages. [Livy, II., 19-20.]

2. FIRST SECESSION OF THE PLEBS. B. C. 494.—For several years after the establishment of the Republic, Rome was continually at war with the neighboring tribes
The burden of these wars was borne by the Plebeians, while all the privileges gained
were enjoyed by the Patricians. The Plebeians complained loudly, but without obtaining any important concessions from the proud Patricians. In 494, returned from
a successful war against the Volsci, the Plebeians refused to lay down their arms, but
seceded in a body to the Mons Sacer, across the Anio, and began to form a new State.
By a fable [Livy, II., 32] Menenius Agrippa was able to persuade the Plebeians to return,
on condition that they should have two magistrates of their own order—"tribunes of
the people."

3. THE PATRICIANS were the *Populus Romanus*, the only class that had any political
privileges. They did not allow intermarriages with foreigners. They were "the
fathers" in Rome, and the head of each clan had a right to a seat in the senate. They
were regarded as the descendants of the earliest tribes in Rome.

4. THE PLEBEIANS.—This class can not be so confidently defined. It is certain
that the Plebs had no political rights, but were free to acquire property and engage in
trade. They were probably those who had come to Rome after the three original
tribes had been established, descendants of the conquered tribes around Rome, and
those who had come to Rome to trade. [And see Lect. II., 4.]

5. TRIBUNES.—Upon the return of the Plebs from the Mons Sacer they were
allowed to elect from among their own order two officers called tribunes. The number
was soon increased to five and then to ten. The tribunes could stop any unjust action
against a Plebeian; could not leave the city further than a mile, must be easily accessible
night and day. They could defend the Plebs but could not initiate any movement in
their favor. [Ihne's *Early Rome*, XIII.]

6. CLIENTS.—The clients formed a numerous class in the later days of the Republic.
Any citizen of Rome became a client by attaching himself personally to some powerful patron who thus became his protector. It came to be a very close and honorable
relation not wholly dependent on blood. But in the earliest days the clients were
perhaps always Plebs.

7. SLAVES.—The slave class was not numerous in Rome till her world-wide conquests brought them in hosts to Italy. They were greatly abused owing to the ease
with which they were obtained. Several times they rose in revolt threatening the
very existence of the State. [Lect. XIX., 2.] The cultivation of the large farms
[Latifundia] of Italy by slave labor ruined the free, small farmers, and became one
important cause of the downfall of Rome.

### LECTURE VII. ROME UNDER THE PATRICIANS.

1. THE SENATE OF THE REPUBLIC.—The Senate was ever the soul of the Republic.
The usual phrase was "Senatus populusque Romanus"—the Senate standing even
before the people. "The Senate had neither executive, legislative nor judicial power.
It was merely a consultative body, free to give advice to the magistrates, when asked
for it, but unable either to give advice unasked or to enforce its acceptance." Its
influence consisted in this, that it really represented the intelligence of the people, and
generally gave a correct expression of the national will. Vacancies were filled by the
consuls—later by the Censors—from ex-magistrates, if there were any, otherwise from
the most influential patricians. [Ihne's *Early Rome*, XI ]

2. POPULAR ASSEMBLIES.—The oldest popular assembly was the Comitia Curiata,
composed entirely of Patricians. From the time of Servius the Comitia Centuriata—
hundred-assembly of both Patricians and Plebeians voting according to wealth—
became more and more influential. The Comitia Tributa was the popular assembly of

the Plebs. Its acts only after long years became binding upon any but Plebs. [Ihne's *Early Rome*, XII.]

3. CORIOLANUS.—In a famine which happened soon after the First Secession of the Plebs, corn was bought for distribution among the people. Later, Gelon sent corn as a present. Coriolanus advised to give the Plebs none till they would give up their tribunes. Hearing this, the Plebs charged him with breaking the peace between the classes, and he fled to the Volscians. Having led a Volscian army within five miles of Rome, he was at last induced to retire, only when his mother, wife and children, at the head of a procession of Roman matrons, begged the safety of Rome. "Thou hast saved Rome, but lost thy son." Livy II., 33-40; Ihne's *Early Rome*, XVI. Plutarch's *Coriolanus*.

4. CINCINNATUS.—In one of their numerous wars with the Æqui, the Romans found themselves in such straits that it was declared that no one but Cincinnatus could save the State. Accordingly, he was made dictator. The committee of notification found him plowing, bare-armed, on his small farm. After some persuasion, he first made his toilet, then received the robes of State, repaired to Rome, and led forth an army. Completely successful, he returned to Rome in triumph, and on the sixteenth day laid down the dictatorship, [which he could have held six months] and returned to his plow. "Honorable poverty."

5. THE TWELVE TABLES. B. C. 451.—In order to get the customs or laws of Rome written down in a code, the Patricians gave up their consuls, the Plebs their tribunes, for one year, and a board of ten [Decemvirs] was created, composed of both Patricians and Plebs. These examined all the codes which they could find, especially Solon's, and toward the end of the year drew off a code of ten tables. But the work was considered unfinished, so they were continued in office and soon added two more tables. Ihne, XVIII.

6. APPIUS CLAUDIUS AND VIRGINIA.—Of the old Decemviral Board, only Appius Claudius was re-elected. He soon became haughty, and the people believed he was about to overthrow the Constitution and establish an oligarchy with himself supreme. Matters were brought to a crisis by the lust of Appius. Virginia, the daughter of a noble Plebeian, was, at his instigation, claimed by a client as his slave. In the trial the bold wickedness of Appius triumphed over justice, and the girl was adjudged to him. Her father, overwhelmed with grief, called her aside for a moment to the booths around the Forum, and there struck her dead at his feet.

7. SECOND SECESSION OF THE PLEBS. B. C. 449.—This outrage led to a second secession, either to the Aventine, the Plebeian stronghold, or to the old place—Mons Sacer. The Decemvirs were obliged to resign, and consuls and tribunes were again elected. By this secession the Plebs appear to have gained practically equal political rights with the Patricians. Livy, II., 34—III., 58.

### LECTURE VIII. CONQUEST OF THE NEIGHBORING TRIBES OF ITALY.

1. CAPTURE OF FIDENAE.—After long years of war with Fidenae [where?] the Romans were at last able to capture the place in a most curious battle. Having attacked the city, they were making good progress, when suddenly the gates were pushed open and there issued, nobody could tell what, bearing innumerable burning brands. For an instant the Romans wavered, but encouraged by the dictator, they sprang to the attack, catching the torches which were thrown, and seizing others; it became literally a battle of fire. The Romans were victorious and the city was destroyed. [Livy, IV., 31–34].

2. CAPTURE OF VEII BY CAMILLUS. B. C. 396.—Veii was across the Tiber twelve miles north of Rome. Strongly built on a hill, it had long withstood the attacks of

Rome. Livy records war after war with apparently no other result than the gradual growth of the city in power. At last the war—for such the thirty years of raids might be called—was terminated by a ten years' siege. [Cf. the Trojan War]. Livy tells [V., 1-23] how, after everything else had failed, a mine was constructed under the fortress to the middle of the city. The Veientes being about to offer sacrifice, the priest declared that whoever should use the animal for omens would be victorious. The Romans in the mine broke through thereupon and carried it off to the dictator—a story which Livy himself does not credit. But the city was taken, the inhabitants sold into slavery, and the spoil, in immense quantities, taken to Rome. [Livy, V., 19-22].

3. THE BATTLE OF THE ALLIA. B. C. 390.—Soon after the destruction of Veii, the Gauls from northern Italy invaded Rome. At the Allia, a small stream flowing into the Tiber about six miles from Rome, the Gauls fairly destroyed the Roman army, and then pushed on to Rome itself almost by the time the news of the disaster arrived.

4. ROME IN RUINS.—The city was taken, except the capitol, which alone was saved by the cackling of the geese sacred to Juno. [Livy, V., 47]. To the rest of the city the torch was applied. Rome destroyed. There had come a turning point in the course of history. What race was to lead the world to law and unity if not Rome? But only the *city* had been destroyed, not ROME. Soon pinched by the famine themselves had created the Gauls began to treat, and presently accepted from the rapidly collecting Romans a heavy ransom. [" Woe to the Vanquished !"] But while the gold was being weighed, Camillus appeared with an army, forcing Brennus and his Gauls to flee. Even then the Romans thought of moving their state to Veii instead of rebuilding on the old site. Plutarch's *Camillus.*

5. MARCUS MANLIUS.—As soon as Rome recovered from the invasion by the Gauls, the Plebeians were again oppressed. The slave barracks were filled with prisoners for debt, Camillus himself treating them very harshly. Then Manlius, who had saved the capitol, took their part. He was at once accused of treason. Tried in the Campus Marcius, he pointed to the capitol which he had saved, and the people acquitted him. Then his persecutors had him tried in a secluded place and obtained sentence. He was thrown from the Tarpeian rock. Livy, VI., 20.

### LECTURE IX. ROMAN POLITICS. [REVIEW.]

1. POLITICAL PARTIES.—It may be said that there were from the earliest times, two quite distinct political parties at Rome. [Livy. Dionysius.]—Patricians and Plebeians. [Lect. VI., 3, 4.] Intelligence, principle, and reason, the true basis of wise political action, had little to do with the politics of ancient Rome. In their passion, heredity, and the blind impulse to maintain one's own order at all hazards were the guiding forces.

2. THE PLEBEIANS RECOGNIZED BY THE STATE.—Romulus is said to have admitted Plebeians into his city. [Lect. II., 3.] Political privileges were first conferred upon them rather indirectly by the Servian Constitution. [Lect. IV., 5.] Though no Pleb might become a magistrate, wealthy Plebs might vote. But Plebs were not allowed any public land, hence their chances for wealth were very limited. Even these privileges were swept away by Tarquinius Priscus under whom the Plebs were little better than slaves.

3. THE FIRST PLEBEIAN MAGISTRATES.—The kings, though patricians, were officials of the whole people, so that the Plebs are little heard of during the monarchy. With the fall of the monarchy, however, we have a new order of things. The Consuls are themselves leaders of the Patrician party, receive the honor direct from the Patricians, and at the end of a single year become private citizens liable to prosecution by new Patrician officers for any act hostile to their order. [E. g., Sp. Cassius, proposer of the first Agrarian law.] [Lec. X., 2.] The Plebs were therefore entirely at the mercy of the

Patricians whose oppressions soon led to the First Secession of the Plebs. [Lect. VI., 2.] Upon this laws were passed (1) protecting the Plebs from usurious interest; (2) granting tribunes; (3) appointing Plebeian aediles—overseers of markets [Lect. VI., 3.] who could protect them from the rapacious patricians. Now for the first time a Plebeian could claim in his own name the protection of law.

4. THE PLEBS GAIN POLITICAL RIGHTS.—Soon after obtaining tribunes and aediles the Plebs "gained the right to summon before their own comitia tributa any one who violated the rights of their order." The Plebiscita—acts of the tributa—did not become binding on their own order till after the enactment of the twelve tables [when?] By the Canulein rogations, B. C. 445, the Plebs gained the right of inter-marriage with Patricians. About the same time the attempt to gain consulship was frustrated by a law permitting, instead of consuls, six military tribunes with consular power who might be either Patrician or Plebeian. At the same time the censorship, a patrician office, was created to receive the most important functions of the consulship.

5. THE PLEBS GAIN POLITICAL EQUALITY.—In 421, by gaining the questorship, Plebeians for the first time entered the Senate. Stolo 367 raised the number of keepers of the Sibyline books from two to ten, half of whom must be Plebeians. He restored the consulship on condition that one must be a Plebeian. The next year Lucius Sextius became the first Plebeian consul. [Livy, VI., 42.] The Patricians retorted by creating the Praetorship to which the most important consular dignities were trans-ferred.

351. Censorship gained.

341. Both consuls *might* be Plebeians.

336. Praetorship gained.          .

300. Office of Pontifex and Augur gained.

286. Third secession of the Plebs. Hortensian laws guaranteed the privileges they had gained, and made the Plebiscita binding on the whole State. There was no longer any political distinction between Patrician and Plebeian.

### LECTURE X. AGRARIAN LAWS.

1. THE PUBLIC LANDS.—By his attempt to grant public lands to Plebeians, Servius incurred the displeasure of the patricians and was soon assassinated. [Lect. IV., 4.] But since public lands came by conquest and Plebeians made up the army, their exclusion appeared more and more unjust. They were first allowed to use the public pastures for a small sum paid to the State, then poor Plebeians were allowed little farms on condition of occupying and defending them. But when the public land—enlarged by conquest—had to be offered to any who could occupy, it necessarily fell to the rich. These preferred slave to free labor [why?] so that the condition of the poor Plebs was pitiable indeed.

2. SPURIUS CASSIUS.—First Agrarian Law. B. C. 486. Spurius Cassius, now consul for the third time, proposed to remedy this injustice by giving half of the land just conquered from the Hernici to the Latins and half to the Plebs. To this he proposed to add other public lands in possession of private citizens. Such monstrous [?] propo-sitions brought the whole Patrician party about his ears. Nothing daunted, he went further and proposed to return to the people the money paid for Sicilian corn. [Lect. VII., 3.] The Agrarian law passed, but was rendered inoperative by Patricians, who the next year tried Cassius and condemned him to death. [Livy, 11., 41–43.]

3. STOLO'S LAW.—More than a century later, [367 (?)] Licinius Stolo, a Plebeian. ten times elected tribune, succeeded in passing a law which limited the land which

might be held by one possessor to five hundred jugera [about 350 acres.] But the Plebs were never able to secure justice in the distribution of the *ager publicus,* though from Stolo's time they appear to have shared its enjoyment. Two and a-half centuries later the Gracchi lost their lives in the same fruitless struggle. [Lect. XIX., 4, 5.] Livy, VI., 42.

## SECTION II. CONQUEST OF ITALY.

### LECTURE XI. THE FIRST SAMNITE WAR.

1. THE SEVEN HILLS.—Roma Quadrata was so called from the shape of the Palatine on which the city of Romulus stood. Gradually the city grew till it occupied the seven hills [Aventine, Capitoline, Cœlian, Esquiline, Viminal, Palatine, Quirinal—forming the acrostic ACCEVPCQ] around which the Servian wall was built.

2. EARLY CONQUESTS.—As soon as the Republic recovered from the stagnation which followed the expulsion of the kings, war and conquest were resumed. By dint of hard fighting and obstinate perseverance the borders of Rome were slowly enlarged. First, Fidenae fell, [Lect. VIII., 1.] then that dangerous rival Veii [Lect. VIII., 2.] Finally, the Æqui, Volsci, and other neighboring tribes with which Rome had carried on an intermittent war from her very foundation were subdued. The borders of Rome now extended southward as far as the Liris. But in a career of conquest there is no stopping point; ever new conquests are required to protect the last.

3. FIRST SAMNITE WAR. B. C. 343-341. Invited by the Campanians to aid them against the Samnites, Rome accepted. She was thus plunged into a conflict which was to last seventy years. In such a hard school was Rome trained to be mistress of the world. After the Romans had gained three victories over the Samnites a peace was concluded by which Rome received Padua, the Samnites, Teanum.

4. OVERTHROW OF THE LATIN CONFEDERACY. 340-338.—The Latin towns to the south and east of Rome had long waged unsuccessful war against the city on the Tiber. But as Rome's hegemony became more firmly established comparative quiet prevailed. At last, however, the whole Latin League, with Caupa and the Volscians as allies, rose against Rome and demanded political equality. [The demand for admission to the consulship and the Senate reminds of the American Revolution and the English Parliament.] Roman victory near Vesuvius. Execution of consul's son for disobediently gaining a victory. [Story of P. Decuis Mus.] Latins overwhelmed at Trifanum. Peace. Latins made citizens without suffrage, *i. e.,* subjects. Antium, whose ship beaks [rostra] were taken to adorn the speaker's platform in the Forum, [hence Rostrum] was made a colony.

### LECTURE XII. SECOND AND THIRD SAMNITE WARS, AND WAR WITH PYRRHUS—TARENTUM.

1. SECOND SAMNITE WAR.—Caudine Pass. B. C. 326-304. Both parties being about to engage in another war [Tarentum. Latins], the first peace between Rome and the Samnites was easily arranged. With the Latins subjected, Rome crossed the Liris and annexed Fregellae, a Samnite town. This was the beginning of a war in which Rome was successful at first, but in 321 the Romans were surrounded at the Caudine Pass, made to surrender, swear to a treaty of peace, and give two nobles as hostages. Whole army passed under the yoke. [What was this form? See Livy, IX., 2-6].

2. CLOSE OF THE WAR.—The Senate refused to ratify the peace, and gave the consuls up to the Samnites, who would not receive them. The Samnites soon driven entirely out of Campania. Etruria and many other neighboring tribes now took part against Rome and checked her progress. Rome again triumphs. Great victory at Vadimonian Lake (310). Nuceria [where ?] falls—attacked by land and sea. First Roman navy (?). With the fall of Boviarum (305) came peace. The Via Flaminia and the Via Valeria now constructed.

3. Third Samnite War. B. C. 398–390.—The Samnites and their allies were soon for the third time at war with Rome. Large armies raised on both sides. Roman victory at Sentinum (395). Samnites finally submit (390). With them the Etruscans, Sabines and others became subject to Rome.

4. War with Pyrrhus–Tarentum. B. C. 282–272.—Roman fleet anchored at Tarentum contrary to an old treaty, was attacked and many crews sold into slavery. Upon approach of Roman army Pyrrhus, king of Epirus, called to assist Tarentum. Pyrrhus victorious at Heraclea (280)—elephants. "Many such victories will ruin me." The next year at Asculum he suffered a like victory. At Beneventum (275) he was completely overthrown and Rome was mistress of Italy.

## Section III.—CONQUEST OF CARTHAGE.

### LECTURE XIII. FIRST PUNIC WAR. B. C. 264.

1. Dido Founds Carthage.—Carthage was founded by Tyre a century before the foundation of Rome (853). Dido was sister of the Tyrian king. Her husband was slain for his great wealth, but Dido, with a company of nobles, escaped with the wealth. Touching at Cyprus she seized a number of maidens for wives to her nobles, and sailed to the African coast. There she bought as much land as could be covered with a bull's hide. Then cutting the hide into the smallest possible strings she surrounded a piece of land large enough for a citadel. [See "Dido," Smith's *Classical Dict.*] There were several Tyrian colonies on this coast before Carthage, but the youngest outstripped them all and became the naval power of the west.

2. Carthage and Rome Compared.—Carthage was a naval power. Rome depended upon her land forces for success. Carthage was a loose confederacy, with little but force or pay to hold her allies. Rome was a fairly compact State with numerous allies bound to her by the strongest ties of sympathy and self-interest. The Carthaginian army was composed of mercenaries; that of Rome of her own citizens and subjects. Perhaps, on the whole, the two powers were pretty evenly matched.

3. Causes of the War.—(1) A deep-seated jealousy between the first sea power and the first land power of the west. (2) Some Campanian allies of Rome took Messana [where?]. Part of the inhabitants appealed to Rome, part to Carthage. The Romans hesitated, but at last sent a force only to find the place already occupied by Carthaginians. They were at once attacked and dislodged. Carthage declared war.

4. In Sicily.—A consul was at once sent to Sicily. Messana was relieved, but an attempt to take Syracuse failed. The next year two Roman armies in Sicily. Hiero, king of Syracuse, went over to the Roman side with his city. Third year Hanno was defeated and Agrigentum taken. Carthage nearly driven out of Sicily.

5. First Naval Victory of the Romans.—Mylae, B. C. 260. The first naval attempt of the Romans failed, but having built a large fleet with boarding bridges [describe these], they next year attacked and destroyed a Carthaginian fleet at Mylae [location?]. Three years later the two navies fought a drawn battle off Tyndaris [where?]

6. Regulus and the Invasion of Africa. B. C. 256–255.—Regulus was one of the consuls for 256. Under the consuls a great army was led into Africa, having first defeated the Carthaginian fleet at Ecnomus [where?] Soon after the landing Regulus was left to conduct the campaign. He defeated the Carthaginians, who sued for peace; failed. Greek mercenaries obtained. The Spartan Xanthippus led them to victory; Regulus captured; sent with an embassy to Rome; persuaded the Senate not to make peace; returned; tortured [chest with spikes?] Art. "Regulus," Smith's *Classical Dict.*

7. ROMAN GAINS.—The Roman fleet sent to rescue the African expedition was on the return destroyed by a storm. Another fleet took Panormus (254), near which three years later the Romans gained an important victory on land. Defeated by sea at Drepanum (249), and long held in check by Hamilcar in Sicily, the Romans at last destroyed the Carthaginian fleet under Hanno, at the Ægatian Islands [location ?] 241.

8. TREATY OF PEACE. B. C. 241.—I. Carthage gave up Sicily. II. Paid 3200 talents ($4,000,000 in ten years).

Rome organized her FIRST PROVINCE, Western Sicily.

## LECTURE XIV. SECOND PUNIC WAR.—HANNIBAL. B. C. 218-202.

1. THE TRUCE. B. C. 240-218.—The brief peace between the first and second Punic wars was scarcely taken seriously by either party. Carthage employed the time in strengthening her resources both by sea and by land. Spain was to replace Sicily, and to this conquest she devoted most of her strength.

2. ROME—SECOND PROVINCE.—Rome, meanwhile, was everywhere active—settling old scores, enlarging her territory. Corsica and Sardinia, formerly dependent upon Carthage, invaded on a flimsy pretext and organized as the SECOND ROMAN PROVINCE.

3. THE ILLYRIANS AND THE GAULS.—The Illyrian pirates punished, and the affairs of Greece interfered with for the first time. [See "The Eastern Civilizations and Greece," Lect. XXV., 5.] Their northern neighbors, the Gauls, whose name, since the fateful day of the Allia, had always inspired the Romans with terror, were vanquished after a hard struggle. They were routed by Flaminius near Telamon [founded by Telamon on his return from the Argonautic expedition?]

4. HANNIBAL. B. C. 247-183.—Son of Hamilcar Barcas, he was taken by his father to Spain, where, at the age of only nine years, he was solemnly led to the altar and made to swear eternal hatred to Rome. To the keeping of that vow, the life of the greatest general of antiquity was devoted. At the death of his brother-in-law, Hasdrubal, he was chosen leader of the Carthaginians in Spain (221). Twenty-six years old, and leader of the only nation able to cope with the Roman Republic! The Carthaginian arms were now rapidly pushed to the Ebro, when Rome protested.

5. SAGUNTUM, B. C. 219.—Hannibal had just ended two successful campaigns against the Spanish savages, and was ready to march against Saguntum, the last stronghold south of the Ebro. He therefore paid no attention to Rome's embassy—scarcely consulted his own government, for although still but twenty-eight years old he was, for military purposes, himself the government. Saguntum was besieged, and after a desperate resistance taken and destroyed. [Livy, XXI, 7-14.]

6. "BEYOND THE ALPS LIES ITALY."—Hannibal, knowing that Rome was fully occupied with their Illyrian and Gaulish neighbors, determined at once upon his course. "It would need but his presence in their midst," he argued, "to enlist not only the Gauls, but most of the Roman allies in Italy under his banner." But to this the Alps interposed the well-nigh insurmountable obstacle of their snowy backs. To a genius less than Hannibal's, this would have been conclusive; but •success smiles at impossibilities. ·

## LECTURE XV. HANNIBAL IN NORTHERN ITALY.

[Follow on a good map the movements of Hannibal.]
1. PASSAGE OF THE ALPS.—[Little St. Bernard Pass?] Starting with a force of 50,000 infantry, 9,000 cavalry and 37 elephants, Hannibal pushed rapidly north, threading his way painfully through the Pyrenees and fighting his way across the Rhone. The hostile tribes living east of Rome were easily dispersed, but continued to annoy his army by sudden attacks, and by rolling down rocks and trees in the narrow passes.

It was only with the greatest difficulty and by the most daring deeds that the passage [Little St. Bernard], occupying fifteen days, was finally accomplished. But Hannibal entered Italy with only 20,000 foot, 6,000 horse and 7 elephants! [Why had he not fought Scipio at the Rhone and taken the easier way by the Mediterranean?]

2. THE TICINUS. B. C. 218.—Hannibal immediately moved southward along the left bank of the Po. Scipio, who having failed to intercept the Carthaginians on the Rhone, had turned back to Italy, was at the same time moving to meet Hannibal. Scipio, having bridged the Ticinus, was leading his cavalry in person when the two generals suddenly faced each other. A brisk skirmish resulted in Hannibal's favor, proving here in this first engagement the superiority of the Carthaginian cavalry. Scipio retired so precipitately and broke down his bridge so hastily as to leave 600 men on the other side to become prisoners. Scipio wounded; Gauls join Hannibal.

3. THE TREBIA. B. C. 218.—A little farther down the Po the Trebia falls into it from the south. Soon after the battle of the Ticinus Hannibal crossed the Po near Placentia [see map] and pushed on after Scipio, who had fortified himself across the Trebia. While Hannibal paused for negotiations with some traitors, Sempronius hurried up from Sicily in forty days and joined Scipio. Sempronius insisted upon a battle; was cautioned by the experience of Scipio, attacked a foraging party with some success and then marched out to meet Hannibal. Without breakfast he led his shivering men through the freezing Trebia against the comfortably-camped and well-fed Carthaginians. The result could not be doubtful. Cool calculation won against precipitate conceit. The Romans were almost annihilated.

4. END OF THE FIRST ITALIAN CAMPAIGN.—Things now looked dark for Rome. Hannibal's first campaign on Italian soil had won for him the cavalry fight on the banks of the Ticinus, the infantry battle on the Trebia, where two consular armies were nearly destroyed, brought over to his standard most of the Gauls, and left him with a greatly strengthened army in full possession of Cisalpine Gaul.

5. PREPARATIONS FOR THE NEXT CAMPAIGN.—At Rome nothing was left undone that could aid the Roman cause. The brave but reckless Flaminius was again made consul with Servilius. Each was placed at the head of an army and early in the spring of 217, sent north to prevent Hannibal's entrance into Roman Italy. The Senate was bent upon the destruction of the invader, and therefore took no notice of the illegal conduct of Flaminius in leaving Rome before his term of office should have begun. Hannibal too was early in the field, for with him everything depended upon celerity.

### LECTURE XVI. THE SECOND CAMPAIGN IN ITALY.

1. BATTLE OF LAKE TRASIMENE. B. C. 217.—As soon as spring opened Hannibal proceeded southward and took up his position on a semi-circular ridge of hills north of Lake Trasimene. [location?] Flaminius following him, was led into a trap. On a foggy morning his troops were passing through the plain, when, after the vanguard had passed the further side, at a signal Hannibal's cavalry attacked them in front while the infantry from ambush administered the most crushing defeat the Romans had yet suffered. Flaminius slain; severe earthquake not noticed by combatants.

2. RESULTS OF TRASIMENE.—The Romans lost fifteen thousand men. Of the prisoners Hannibal at once released the allies of Rome as a bribe to induce their cities to join the Carthaginians. In this appeared Hannibal's hope of conquering Rome—he counted on her allies coming to his standard. Rome was in consternation; "We have been defeated in a great battle!" An immediate attack was expected. An army was hastily collected and the city put into the best possible condition for defense.

3. HANNIBAL'S NEXT MOVEMENTS.—But Hannibal instead of marching on Rome turned northward toward Spoletium [location]. That city would not join him, so he

passed on into Picenum to the Adriatic and opened communication by sea with Carthage. Having rested through the heat of summer he pushed southward in the fall "plundering as he went." Striving to bring on a battle he plundered the rich Falernian plains. Hemmed in; cleared a pass by oxen with burning fagots tied to their horns. [Lect. VIII., 1.] Went into winter quarters near Cannae.

4. ROMAN IMPATIENCE.—After Trasimene, a Dictator was demanded. Quintus Fabius [Cunctator] appointed. Follows Hannibal at safe distance but refuses to be drawn into an engagement. Rome impatient. The next consuls, Varro and Æmilius, chosen to fight Hannibal. Æmilius a good general. Varro too rash.

5. BATTLE OF CANNAE. B. C. 216.—It was only necessary for Hannibal's overthrow to continue the policy of Fabius; but Varro, over confident, insisted upon attacking Hannibal. On a day when affairs fell to his direction he decided for battle. The Romans, in their careless haste, allowed themselves to be again surrounded by the Carthaginians, and their force annihilated. The Roman loss exceeded 40,000. Among the slain were Æmilius and eighty men of senatorial rank. Cannae was the climax of Carthaginian success, of Roman disaster. Capua surrenders to Hannibal, who winters there.

6. CONDUCT OF THE SENATE.—Now were displayed those qualities which so distinguished the Roman Senate. The gates were shut, only thirty days allowed for mourning, and every available recruit brought into the army. Hannibal's ambassadors were not even allowed to enter the city. "Rome will never treat with a victorious enemy." Hannibal himself rode up to the walls, but did not attack the city.

### LECTURE XVII. FROM CANNAE TO METAURUS. B. C. 216-207.

1. ROME ON THE DEFENSIVE.—The terrible disaster at Cannae more than vindicated the cautious policy of the mild but courageous Fabius, who was now recalled to the leadership of the Roman forces—a trust which he discharged with distinction for several years. The Senate ordered the survivors of Cannae to Sicily, where they could have no chance to wipe off their disgrace, and disfranchised those who had been inclined to forsake the republic. Rome's policy was henceforth that of the Cunctator. This was merely an open acknowledgment that Rome's infantry was no match for Hannibal's.

2. HANNIBAL'S FIRST DEFEAT—Nola. B. C. 215.—The war was now confined to Southern Italy. The Italians who had gone over to Hannibal he found it exceedingly difficult to protect. With three Roman armies watching him [with a view chiefly to keeping out of his way], Hannibal could not relieve the cities friendly to him as rapidly as they were attacked by the Romans. At last, in an attack upon Nola, which had been occupied by a Roman army under Marcellus, a well-directed sally cut off a Carthaginian contingent and forced Hannibal to retire. Winter quarters. On the defensive.

3. SPAIN.—With Hannibal cooped up in Southern Italy, Rome could spare some forces for Spain. Thither the two Scipios were sent. They defeated Hannibal's brother, Hasdrubal, and pushed on to the Gaudalquivir, where they defeated the Carthaginians in two battles, and continued to maintain themselves there for several years.

4. TARENTUM. B. C. 212.—Soon after Cannae, Hannibal had appeared before Tarentum expecting aid from Philip V. of Macedonia, and also that the city gates would be opened to him. He was disappointed in both, and was compelled to retire. Some time after this he again moved on Tarentum. Two Greeks, under pretense of hunting, daily visited his camp and arranged to admit him to the city on a night when the Roman general would surely be engaged in drunken revel. The treachery succeeded, and Tarentum passed into the hands of Hannibal.

5. First Macedonian War  B. C. 215–206.  Philip V., of Macedonia, had promised
to aid Hannibal against Tarentum.  Their letters were intercepted by the Romans and
a fleet sent to prevent the fulfillment of the promise.  As soon as she could spare the
forces Rome proceeded to punish Philip.  Rome formed a league led by the Ætolians
against Philip.  Several years of indecisive war—favorable to Rome—led to a
reluctant peace.

6. Syracuse Taken by the Romans. B. C. 212.—The war raged hotter and hotter
in Sicily.  The Romans were besieging Syracuse; the Carthaginians trying to relieve
it.  Marcellus destroyed Hamilcar's army.  Brave resistance of Syracuse aided by the
inventive genius of Archimedes.  City taken and plundered.

7. Capua Taken by Rome. B. C. 211.—The next year witnessed the fall of the only
important Italian city which had early gone over to Hannibal.  The Romans besieged
Capua closely, and Hannibal, in an attempt to relieve the city, was repulsed.  His
march on Rome.  Failed.  Capua taken; fifty-three citizens beheaded; many sold into
slavery.

8. Battle of the Metaurus. B. C. 207.—At length Hasdrubal, meeting with little
success in Spain, determined to follow Hannibal into Italy and join him there.  The
Romans were greatly alarmed at this news.  Twenty-three legions raised.  The consuls directed to make every effort to prevent the meeting of the two brothers.  Hasdrubal's dispatches intercepted.  Hannibal's march.  Drawn battle in Lucania.  The
consul Nero leaves part of his army to watch Hannibal, and takes the rest by forced
marches to join his colleague in the north.  The junction effected.  Hasdrubal's army
destroyed and himself killed on the Metaurus, B. C. 207.  Hasdrubal's bloody head
thrown to the Carthaginian pickets apprised Hannibal that his hope of success in Italy
was gone.  [Creasy's *Decisive Battles.  IV.*]

9. End of War.—After Metaurus it was a mere question of time with Hannibal.
Meanwhile Rome pushed the war in Africa.  Hannibal was recalled to meet Scipio,
and at Zama [location], B. C. 202, the Carthaginian army was annihilated.

10. Peace.—Carthage required to (1) surrender Spain and the islands of the Mediterranean ; (2) transfer kingdom of Syphax to Massinissa ; (3) annual tribute of 200
talents ($250,000) for fifty years ; (4) surrender all warships but ten ; (5) no war to be
undertaken without consent of Rome.

## Section IV.  CONQUEST OF THE EAST.

### LECTURE XVIII.  MACEDONIA, ANTIOCHUS III., CARTHAGE.

1. Battle of Cynoscephalae. B. C. 197.  Scarcely had Rome received the news
of Zama before she had plunged into new wars.  Transpadane, [across the Po] Italy
was, by hard fighting, again subdued.  Then Philip V. was punished for aiding Hannibal at Zama.  His army was routed in the battle of Cynoscephalæ; Philip was deposed
from the hegemony of Greece, and his kingdom made dependent upon Rome.

2. Antiochus III. of Syria.—After Zama, Hannibal made his way to the court of
Antiochus.  This and the meddling of Antiochus in Grecian affairs led to war with
Rome.  Antiochus entered Greece and occupied Thermopylæ.  Hannibal himself led
a fleet which was defeated at the Eurymedon.  Soon the war was pushed into Asia,
and at Magnesia (190) Antiochus was defeated and made practically dependent upon
Rome.  Hannibal escaped, but in B. C. 183 took poison to avoid capture.

3. Battle of Pydna. B. C. 168—Perseus, son of Philip V., plotted revenge upon
Rome.  The Senate, informed of this, at once sent an army into Macedonia.  For some
time the Romans made but little progress; then Æmilius Paullus was sent out; the

army thoroughly reorganized, and a battle fought at Pydna, in which the army of Perseus was destroyed. Macedonia was dismembered, the rebels cruelly punished, and the country subjected—one thousand Greeks carried off to Rome, among whom was the historian, Polybius.

4. CORINTH DESTROYED. B. C. 146.—About twenty years later a rising of the Achean League ("The Eastern Civilizations and Greece," Lect. XXV., 4) led to the destruction of its leading city. Some of the exiles (Sec. 3) had been allowed to return, and these immediately stirred up a rash revolt, which resulted in the destruction of Corinth. ("The Eastern Civilizations and Greece," Lect. XXV., 5).

5. DESTRUCTION OF CARTHAGE. B. C. 146.—The Third Punic War was caused by Roman jealousy and fear really, but, nominally, because Carthage made war without the consent of Rome [Lect. XVII., 10] Massinissa's attacks [prompted by Rome?] Carthage met, first, by appeal to Rome [without result,] then by battle. But Rome's course had been determined beforehand by Cato's oft repeated "Delenda est Carthago." So rapidly had Carthage recovered after the Second Punic War, that her very existence was believed to be a menace to Rome. Carthaginians beseiged; brave resistance; arms treacherously taken by the Romans; women cut off their hair for catapult strings; the men fashion new arms. City at last taken and burned; conflagration seventeen days, and a plow run over the site.

6. ROMAN PROVINCES.—At this time Rome had eight provinces—(1) Sicily, [First Punic War;] (2) Sardinia and Corsica, [Invasion contrary to treaty with Carthage;] (3) Hither Spain (4) Farther Spain, [Second Punic War;] (5) Cisalpine Gaul, [Subjection of the Gauls;] (6) Illyricum, [Battle of Pydna;] (7) Macedonia and Greece, [Destruction of Corinth;] (8) Africa, [Destruction of Carthage.]

7. GOVERNMENT OF THE PROVINCES.—The first four provinces had been governed by praetors—judges whose duty it was to preside over the courts. After that all six of the praetors were kept in the city, and at the termination of their year of office they were sent by lot to the provinces as pro-praetors. But warlike provinces were governed by pro-consuls—consuls, i. e., after their year office. Hence pro-consular and pro-praetorial provinces. No more dictators. "The consuls shall take measures for the public good according to their discretion."

SECTION V.   TENDING TOWARDS EMPIRE.

**LECTURE XIX. ROME AND THE TEUTONIC PEOPLES.**

1. NUMANTIA DESTROYED. B. C. 133.—The Spanish tribes were ever restless and fierce. Roman arms alone kept them in subjection. Variathus, the most dangerous Spanish leader, waged incessant war till he was murdered, when Numantia became the seat of the war. At last Scipio was sent against the city. After a brave resistance of fifteen months it yielded and was destroyed. Scipio Numanticus.

2. FIRST SERVILE WAR. B C. 135-132.—Conquest had made slaves so plentiful in Rome that they were very harshly treated. A slave more or less made little difference one way or another. Under a slave, who called himself King Antiochus, the slaves of Sicily revolted and were only put down by the help of Roman armies. Eunus, the leader, was executed also with a large number of slaves.

3. DEPRAVITY FOLLOWS CONQUEST.—From the close of the Second Punic War Greek learning, philosophy and literature gained rapidly at Rome. All the earliest historians of Rome were Greeks—Fabius Pictor, Polybius, Dionysius. Greek revels of the Bacchanalia. Luxury. Loss of political honor. Bribery. A few noble families control affairs. Corrupt family life. All these things were but a natural consequence of Rome's rapid progress in wealth and power with a low moral standard.

4. TIBERIUS GRACCHUS. B. C. 133.—Increase of great plantations [Latifundia] worked by slaves led to loud complaints from the small farmers who were crushed out. Gracchus, a plebeian, as tribune proposed a revival of the Licinian law restricting land holdings to 500 jugera [Lect. X., 3], except he would allow 250 jugera extra to each son. Law adopted. Gracchus next proposed to popular assembly, instead of the Senate, the division of the spoil of Pergamus. Upon an unconstitutional attempt to obtain the tribunate again he was murdered by a mob.

5. CAIUS GRACCHUS. B. C. 123.—The younger brother of Tiberius, and greatly his superior. Elected to the tribunate against the will of the Senate. At once he set about reforms which looked to the complete overthrow of existing conditions. [Did Gracchus expect to become sole Ruler of Rome—i. e., the head of the nominal democracy?] Re-elected tribune next year, he took away the privilege of jury duty from the senators and gave it to the order next below senatorial rank. Many public questions—colonization—he refused to submit to the Senate. Not elected the third time; civil strife brought on a conflict between his followers and the optimates. Gracchus and three thousand of his followers slain.

6. WAR WITH JUGURTHA. B. C. 111-105.—Adopted by a son of Massinissa. Got possession of the kingdom by bribing the Romans sent to divide it. Bribed a consul to obtain peace. Not ratified. Jugurtha invited to Rome on promise of safe conduct. Made partisans by buying men of influence. But when he allowed [instigated?] the murder in Rome itself of the last possible rival to his throne he was sent away and war renewed. Romans suffered a humiliating defeat—sent under the yoke. Marius sent out. Gained several victories and finally conquered Jugurtha himself who starved in a Roman prison. Peace.

7. FIRST INVASION OF THE TEUTONIC PEOPLE. B. C. 102.—For about ten years the Cimbri and Teutones had been fighting, and often defeating, the Roman armies in Gaul and Spain. At last these two nations of barbarians agreed to enter Italy in two bands. Marius again elected consul and continued in the office five years. The Teutones were met by Marius at Aquae Sextae and their army annihilated. Then hurrying across the Alps, he, with his colleague, met and annihilated the Cimbri·at Vercellae. "The Teutons have all the land they need on the other side of the Alps." Important changes in the constitution of the army.

### LECTURE XX. WARS, FOREIGN AND CIVIL.

1. THE SOCIAL WAR. B. C. 90-88.—A second rising of slaves in Sicily was put down by Marius after four years of hard fighting. Marius now became haughty and unpopular at Rome. In his absence the tribune Drusus brought forward three laws: (1) Reform of judicial department; (2) New division of lands; (3) Conferring of citizenship on the Italians. Drusus assassinated. The Italians—most of Italy, except Rome itself—make war. The Marsians in the north defeated by Marius, but elsewhere the Romans were less successful and other tribes were about to revolt. Citizenship granted to the Latins who had remained faithful. Rome finally victorious. Citizenship granted to all Latins who applied for it.

2. MITHRIDATES. B. C. 88-84.—An Eastern Monarch. Kingdom of the Bosphorus around the Black Sea. Sulla, proconsul of Cilicia, had fought against him. War declared. Mithridates defeats the king of Bythinia. Joined by Greek cities of Asia-Minor which in one day put to death all their Latin inhabitants. Mithridates defeated by Sulla at Chaeronea in 86, at Orchomenus in 85. The next year Sulla marched through Thrace into Asia-Minor and forced Mithridates to conclude a humiliating peace.

3. THE CIVIL WAR.—Marius and Sulla, B. C. 88-82. Meanwhile the democratic party had tried to deprive Sulla of power and appoint Marius in his place. Sulla

marched upon Rome, took the city by storm, and slew the democratic leaders, except Marius, who escaped to Africa. Sulla returns to the Mithridatic war. Marius in his turn takes Rome and slaughters all optimates who had not fled. Marius consul seventh time. His death, B. C. 86.

4. SULLA'S PROSCRIPTIONS.—Upon Sulla's return to Italy in 83 he landed in Brundisium with a large army and began the overthrow of the Marian party now led by young Marius and Carbo. After several hard battles and dreadful punishments inflicted upon conquered cities by Sulla, young Marius ordered himself killed by his slaves. Sulla then entered Rome and had himself appointed Dictator for an unlimited time. Reign of terror. Lists of the doomed posted—in all four thousand seven hundred—[lex de proscribendis malis civibus.] In 79 Sulla resigned the Dictatorship and the next year died.

5. THIRD SERVILE WAR.—Gladiators, B. C. 73–71. Gladiators escaped from training school at Capua, took refuge in the crator of Vesuvius, and from there, under the command of Spartacus, plundered the neigboring lands. Reinforced by slaves, they became an army and threatened Rome. Finally defeated by Crossus and their remnants annihilated by Pompey.

6. POMPEY.—The Pirates Suppressed, B. C. 67. Rome's neglect of her fleet led to a rapid increase of piracy in the Mediterranean. With headquarters at Crete and Cilicia the pirates controlled the whole sea and became very troublesome, capturing merchant ships at will. For ten years a desultory and ineffectual war had been waged against them, but in 67 B. C., Pompey was given unlimited command for three years over the Mediterranean and its coasts fifty miles inland. Two short campaigns were enough. Great numbers of ships were captured, the pirates slain or colonized inland, and their strongholds destroyed.

7. OVERTHROW OF MITHRIDATES. B. C. 74–64.—Mithridates had never ceased to give trouble in Asia Minor in spite of the peace. Now he marched into Bythinia and declared war. The Romans fought several battles [Tigranocerta] with him. Then Pompey was given command in Asia with unlimited powers. Won night battle on the Lycos. Flight of Mithridates. Asia Minor organized as a province. Mithridates, in the midst of elaborate preparations for an invasion of Rome, hears of the revolt of his son, Pharnaces, and slays himself.

8. CATILINE'S CONSPIRACY. B. C. 66–62.—Democrats, led by Crassus and Julius Cæsar, unite with the worst element in Rome to overthrow the optimates before the return of Pompey, whose unlimited power they dreaded. The first conspiracy was to murder the consuls, make Crassus dictator and Cæsar his master of horse. Failed. Next plot, to make Catiline consul, backed by Cæsar and Crassus. Succeeded, but with Cicero for colleague. Catiline's plot to burn the city failed. His plot to murder his competitors and Cicero revealed by spies and denounced by Cicero in the Senate. Orations against Catiline. Conspirators strangled without trial. Catiline fell in battle. Cicero's *Orations against Catiline ;* Plutarch's *Cicero.*

## SECTION VI.—THE STRUGGLE FOR SUPREMACY.

### LECTURE XXI. THE FIRST TRIUMVIRATE.

1. JULIUS CÆSAR.—Of patrician birth himself, Cæsar espoused the cause of the commons. He married the daughter of Cinna; escaped Sulla's proscriptions, though he had to leave Rome; was thought to be privy to Catiline's plot; spoke in Senate against the execution of the plotters, but all the time increased in popular favor. Elected aedile in 65, he went deeply in debt for shows and public entertainments. In 62, while he was praetor, Crassus paid off part of his debts and procured for him the pro-praetorship of Spain. In this office he both paid his heavy obligations and won military glory. Plutarch's *Julius Cæsar.*

2. CRASSUS.—The wealthiest man of Rome (?)  He had been consul in B. C. 70.
United with Cæsar and Pompey, B. C. 60, to form the first triumvirate.  In B. C. 57
was made pro-consul of Syria, one of the richest of the provinces.  Killed four years
later in an expedition against the Parthians.  [Molten gold poured down his throat?]

3. POMPEY.—The third member of the triumvirate and Cæsar's son-in-law.  He
first attracted public notice in his campaign with Sulla against the Marians.  [Lect.
XIX., 4].  At the age of twenty-five he returned from successful wars in Sicily and
Africa, for which he received the title " Great."  He also fought successfully in Spain;
cut off the remnant of the gladiators; crushed the pirates in the Mediterranean; was
consul with Crassus in 70, and after Sulla's death was the most powerful man in Rome.

4. THE TRIUMVIRATE FORMED. B. C. 60.—The events described had brought Cæsar,
Pompey and Crassus into rather intimate relations.  But neither was willing to yield
to the other in the matter of supremacy.  When, therefore, the Senate refused to
divide certain public lands among Pompey's men he proceeded to form with Cæsar and
Crassus an alliance which should virtually control the affairs of Rome.  The next year
they procured the consulship for Cæsar and practically forced the Senate to make him
the almost independent governor of both the Gauls and Illyricum.

5. CÆSAR IN GAUL. B. C. 58–51.—The next few years discovered in Cæsar perhaps
the greatest, certainly the most successful, general the world had yet seen.  He subjected all Gaul [and France bears to-day the marks of that subjection—in church and
language] to the Roman yoke.  He twice invaded Britain in 55 and 54 and pushed far
into the German forests across the Rhine.  In all these years of warfare with savages
he, perhaps, never lost a battle.  [Cæsar's Commentaries.]

6. RESULTS OF THE CONQUEST OF GAUL.—(1) "Celtic nation destroyed—completely
Romanized.  (2) Establishment of a barrier, which for four hundred years protected
Rome against the barbarians.  (3) Enlarged the boundaries of the old world by adding
the territory of Gaul and some knowledge of Britain and Germany.  (4) Furnished the
means for the necessary change from republic to monarchy."

THE BATTLE OF PHARSALUS. B. C. 48.—The death of Crassus in Mesopotamia in 53
destroyed the balance in the triumvirate.  About the same time Cæsar's daughter,
Julia, Pompey's wife, died.  Cæser and Pompey rapidly became estranged, and in 49
Cæsar determined upon war.  The Rubicon [where?] Spain overrun, and Pompey's
army driven from Italy.  Cæsar followed across Epirus into Thessaly.  At Pharsalus,
B. C. 48, Pompey's army was annihilated—20,000 made prisoners—Cæsar's army num-
bered only 22,000.  Cæsar was supreme; he had all but the title of king.  Strong
opposition; continual war.

### LECTURE XXII.  LATER WARS AND DEATH OF CÆSAR.

1. CÆSAR SUPREME.—After the disaster at Pharsalus Pompey fled to Egypt, where
he was murdered.  This left Cæsar without a rival.  At Rome he was made consul for
five years, tribune for life and dictator for one year.

2. THE ALEXANDRINE WAR. B. C. 48–47.—Cæsar followed Pompey to Egypt, where
he found Cleopatra and her brother contending against each other.  Cæsar readily
decided in favor of Cleopatra.  Upon this the people of Alexandria rose and besieged
him in his palace, afterwards in Pharos, with greatly superior force.  Once had to swim
for life from a sinking boat.  At last reinforced, easily beat the Egyptians in the open
field.

3. PHARNACES DEFEATED. B. C. 47.—Son of Mithridates.  King of Pontus, Asia
Minor, and other districts.  Leaving Egypt under a Roman garrison, Cæsar went to
Asia Minor, defeated Pharnaces at Zela, reorganized Asia, and then set out for Rome.
Pharnaces was killed in a battle with a revolted governor.

4. AFRICAN WAR. B. C. 47-46.—Cæsar next undertook war against young Pompey, Scipio, Cato and other Pompeians who had taken post with King Juba, in Africa; Cæsars rash landing. After small battles, Cæsar was completely victorious in the battle of Thapsus. In all, 50,000 of the enemy were put to death. Scipio and Cato committed suicide; Juba had himself killed by his slaves. Cæsar, upon his return to Rome, celebrated four triumphs, for Gaul, Egypt, Pharnaces and Africa.

5. FALL OF POMPEY'S SONS. B. C. 46-45.—Young Pompey escaped from Africa and joined his brother in Spain. Cæsar was at first repulsed by the brothers, but afterwards they were overthrown and one was slain in the battle of Munda [location?] Cæsar had now literally conquered the world.

6. CÆSAR'S POWERS. B. C. 45 —Upon his return to Rome Cæsar forced the Senate to appoint him consul, dictator and censor for life. "He was possessed of the imperium which gave him full control of the finances and military affairs of the State. As censor he could enlarge the Senate; as Pontifex Maximus he controlled religious affairs; as [practically] tribune he had the initiative in legislation and was the sacred protector of the people. The Senate was increased to 900 members, but lost all real power." The government was still administered under the old forms, but Cæsar held all the offices!

7. CÆSAR ASSASSINATED. B. C. 44, MCH. 15.—The opposition finally developed a plot against Cæsar's life. On the 15th of March it chanced that the Senate was to meet in the theatre of Pompey. As Cæsar entered he was met by a group apparently wishing to present petitions, but just as he came opposite the statue of Pompey he was slain. [The spirit of the times is very well reflected in Shakespeare's *Julius Cæsar*.]

### LECTURE XXIII. THE SECOND TRIUMVIRATE.

1. MARK ANTONY.—Cæsar's nephew, son of his Sister Julia. Early lost his father. Step-father put to death by Cicero, as one of Catiline's conspirators. Dissolute. Fought in Syria and in Egypt in 55. In the civil war he was a strong partisan of Cæsar; fought at Pharsalus; was consul with Cæsar in 44 when he offered his uncle the kingly crown at a festival. At Cæsar's death held his money and papers and tried in vain to succeed him. Plutarch's *Mark Antony*.

2. LEPIDUS.—Praetor when the war between Cæsar and Pompey broke out. Joined Cæsar's party. Consul fled, leaving him highest magistrate in Italy. Consul with Cæsar in 46. At Cæsar's death he was near the city with an army collected for service in Spain and Gaul. Aided Antony in conflict with Senate. Later when Antony fled to him in Gaul he was declared a public enemy by the senate, and both straightway marched with a strong army into Italy, where they were joined by Octavius, and the Second Triumvirate was formed.

3. OCTAVIUS, AFTERWARDS AUGUSTUS. Grandson of Cæsar's Sister Julia. Cæsar's grand-nephew—early lost his father. When four years old adopted by Cæsar. Educated by his grandmother, Julia, and carefully watched by his great-uncle. Early sent by him to the camp at Appolonia [location?] to learn military affairs. At Cæsar's death he set out for Italy, where he learned of Cæsar's wish that he should succeed him. Opposed by Antony. Compelled senate to make him consul. Marched north professedly against Antony, with whom he became reconciled, and the Third Triumvirate was formed. Ratified by people for five years.

4. BATTLE OF PHILIPPI. B. C. 42.—The Triumvirs celebrated their assumption of power by putting to death over 2,000 of the opposite party, among them Cicero. [How had he offended Antony?] They then made war upon the republican party, whose leaders made a stand at Philippi [location?] Here the Triumvirs were victorious in two battles. The republican leaders, Cassius and Brutus, committed suicide. Antony ravaged Asia, and then followed Cleopatra, who met him at Tarsus [where?], to Egypt. Octavius, in Italy, distributing land to the veterans.

6. PERUSINE WAR. B. C. 41-40.—Antony's wife, Fulvia, was ambitious, and, not having been permitted to go with her husband, she determined to check the power of Octavianus in Italy. She and a brother of Antony's raised their standard at Praeneste. Obliged to retire, they took refuge in Perusia, where the next year they surrendered, on condition that the leaders should be spared. Death of Fulvia. Antony marries sister of Octavius. The world was then parcelled out—Antony the East; Octavius the west; Lepidus, Africa. Antony with Cleopatra.

6. THE SICILIAN WAR. B. C. 38-36.—Pompey's son, who had established a maritime power in Sicily, now cut off Rome's supply of corn, and war resulted. Octavius lost several fleets in vain, but then he gave Agrippa full power to conduct the war. With great resolution Agrippa made a harbor [how?], created a fleet, and conquered Pompey. Meanwhile Antony and Octavius had patched up a new difficulty; the Triumvirate received an extension of five years.

7. BATTLE OF ACTIUM. B. C. 36.—But matters soon came to a crisis. Antony gave Roman land to Cleopatra, and sent his wife [sister of Octavius] papers of divorce. Octavius declared war against Cleopatra The movement of Antony and Cleopatra to Greece. Actium [where?] Met by the fleet of Octavius under Agrippa. Fierce battle. Before it was decided Cleopatra fled; Antony followed. The Roman Republic no longer existed, even in name. Octavius given the title AUGUSTUS. [Cf. Pharaoh, Caliph, Sultan, Czar]. See for the spirit of the times Shakespeare's *Antony and Cleopatra*.

---

## PART III.—THE EMPIRE. [OUTLINE HINTS.]

---

### LECTURE XXIV.

1. THE REPUBLIC CONVERTED INTO AN EMPIRE. B. C. 31.—From the time of Julius Cæsar Rome had been an Empire in all but name. Soon after Actium the Imperial dignities were granted to Octavius, though even then the senate would not go further than Augustus [*i. e.*, "illustrious," "sublime"—Cf. "Sublime Porte,"] in the matter of a title. He enjoyed the powers for the acquisition of which Cæsar had been slain; reduced the senate to 600. Standing body-guard the Praetorian Cohorts—beginning of the direct influence of the army. Golden age in literature—Virgil, Horace, Ovid, Catullus, and many others.

2. REIGN OF AUGUSTUS [SECOND CÆSAR]. B. C. 31—14 A.D.—Almost the first act of Augustus was to make a tour of the East. Friends rewarded, enemies punished. He conducted expeditions against the Parthians, others in Spain, and numerous campaigns against the Germans, who were becoming troublesome. Franchise extended over Italy. Census and compilation of his "Breviarium." Defeat of Varus in the Teutoburg forest by Arminius, 9 A.D. Wise Ruler. Empire prosperous. Augustus adopted his stepson.

3. TIBERIUS [THIRD CÆSAR]. A.D. 14-37.—Succeeded Octavius without opposition. Revolts in the army; armies of the Rhine under Germanicus, nephew of Tiberius, hardly kept loyal. Election of magistrates taken from popular assemblies and given to senate. Tiberius put to death the last rival for his throne, and later Germanicus, (?) because of his influence with the army. Sejanus, the real ruler. Poisoned Tiberius' son, Drusus. Tiberius retires to Caprae, and the monster Sejanus revels in tyranny and blood. Unites the Praetorians around Rome, the foundation of their future power. Selfish tyrant.

4. CALIGULA [BOOTS] 37-41, AND CLAUDIUS 41-54.—(1) Son of the Germanicus, who was slain by Tiberius, dubbed "caligula" by the soldiers from his peculiar foot-gear.

Cruel, half-crazy monster. Murdered. (2) Succeeded by his uncle, Claudius. Weak; ruled by favorites. Put his wife to death; ruled by second wife, Agrippina, daughter of Germanicus, who persuaded him to adopt her son Nero instead of his first wife's son. When Claudius repented she poisoned him. Conquest of Britain—made a province.

5. NERO—LAST OF THE CÆSARS. 54–68.—Educated by Seneca. If it were possible to paint such a character too black, perhaps Nero has suffered that treatment. If Nero was all that was bad it must be remembered that he was the product of his times. With a father of such flimsy stuff as Claudius, a mother of such calculating blood-thirstiness as Agrippina, and a people from whom the sense of honor and self-respect had departed, what is the very best that could be demanded of Nero? He poisoned his step-brother; had his mother put to death; drove his wife from him and lived with his freedwoman, Acte; married Poppaea, and in a passion gave her a kick, from which she died; had a death sentence for any who opposed his whim; drove a chariot in the games; acted and sang on the stage; burnt Rome (?) to make room for his proposed palace; charged the crime to the Jews and Christians—the same to the Romans—and began the First Persecution of the Christian, in which Paul certainly, Peter perhaps, lost his life.

6. THE FLAVIAN EMPERORS.—These inhuman orgies were finally stopped by a revolt in Gaul [Nero fled and killed himself] led by Galba, who was proclaimed Emperor. Soldiers murdered him after seven months and proclaimed Otho. Vitellius proclaimed by another section of the army. Then the legions in Syria proclaimed their leader, Vespasian (69–79), who, by his own address, became a real emperor. Revolt of the Jews put down by his son Titus. Jerusalem destroyed 70 A.D. Vespasian was succeeded by his two sons; first Titus 79–81, then Domitian 81–96. Agricola in Britain. Recalled. Poisoned (?). Domitian was a cruel tyrant. Second persecution of Christians.

7. AGE OF THE ANTONINES.—Domitian was murdered. Succeeded by Nerva 96–98, whom the murderers proclaimed. Adopted Trajan who succeeded him (98–117). Widest extent of the empire. Wars with Parthians and Dacians. Column of Trajan. Adopted Hadrian (117–138). Progress through all the empire. Peace. Abandoned the most distant provinces in Asia. Succeeded by Antonius Pius (138–161), and he by Marcus Aurelius (161–180). Border wars. Wrote his "Meditations" at intervals in his tent on the German frontier.

## LECTURE XXV. FALL OF THE WESTERN EMPIRE. 476 A.D.

1. FROM THE ANTONINES TO DIOCLETIAN. (180–284).—M. Aurelius was succeeded by his profligate son Commodus (180–192). Paid tribute to the Germans, gave the government to the Praetorians, was murdered; succeeded by Pertinax, Julian and Septimus Severus in one year. Severus reigned eighteen years, died in Britain, and was succeeded by Caracalla (211–217). Citizenship conferred on all the provinces so that higher tax might be extorted. Murdered. The next seventy years a period of anarchy. Reins of government held by one man only so long as he could keep out of the reach of a stronger competitor.

2. DIOCLETIAN. (284–305).—Proclaimed by the soldiers. Empire divided into (1) East, with a capital at Nicomedia [where?] ruled by Diocletian; and (2) West, capital chiefly at Milan, ruled by co-Augustus, Maximian. Each Augustus was to be assisted by a Cæsar. General persecution of Christians: Resigned and compelled Maximian to do the same. General disorganization. Constantine, in Britain, succeeded to power.

3. CONSTANTINE. (306–337.)—Called the Great. Long struggle with rivals for the throne. Sole ruler in 323. Almost his first act as sole ruler was to issue an edict making Christianity practically the State religion. Called the church council of

Nicaea.   First Ecumenical Council.   Nicene creed.   Arianism declared heresy.   [Find all about Arianism.]   Divided the Empire finally and made Byzantium (afterwards Constantinople) the capital.   From this time dates the rapid increase in power of the Roman Bishop—[Popes?]

4.  INVASION OF TEUTONIC TRIBES.  375 A. D.—From Constantine's time there was a nominal emperor in the West and another in the East.   Disorder prevailed everywhere.   At last the West Goths [consult map] pushed across the Danube into the Eastern Empire.   Battle of Adrianople (378).   The nominal emperor then made a barbarian, Theodosius (379), co-regent—real ruler.

5.  FALL OF THE WESTERN EMPIRE.  476 A. D.—Things came rapidly to a crisis at Rome.   The soldiers had for years been the real rulers, though they preferred to be so through a nominal emperor.   But in 476 the throne fell to a useless boy, Odovaker. A barbarian deposed him and sent the insignia of office to Zeno, Emperor at Constantinople.   In return he was made Patrician of Rome.   Under this title he continued to govern the Western Empire for the Emperor at Constantinople.   Note how small a change in the real condition—only that of name.   Rome's life was perpetuated and transmitted in (1) Language; (2) Church; (3) Law.